> To Rosie, Anne, Marie Bailey
> on your Christening Day
> Sunday 26th February 2017
> Love from
> Sally, Pete & A
> xxx

The Adventures of
Roy and Rosie Rabbit

Alan Stephenson

Illustrated by: Su Stephenson

AuthorHouse™
1663 Liberty Drive
Bloomington, IN 47403
www.authorhouse.com
Phone: 1-800-839-8640

© 2011 Alan Stephenson. All Rights Reserved.

No part of this book may be reproduced, stored in a retrieval system,
or transmitted by any means without the written permission of the author.

First published by AuthorHouse 08/292011

ISBN: 978-1-4567-9728-7 (sc)

Printed in the United States of America

Any people depicted in stock imagery provided by Thinkstock are models,
and such images are being used for illustrative purposes only.
Certain stock imagery © Thinkstock.

This book is printed on acid-free paper.

Because of the dynamic nature of the Internet, any web addresses or links contained in this book may have changed since publication and may no longer be valid. The views expressed in this work are solely those of the author and do not necessarily reflect the views of the publisher, and the publisher hereby disclaims any responsibility for them.

These stories have been created by myself and my wonderful grandchildren, whilst out walking across the fields.

We do have some lovely times.

For Gemma, Lea, Alex, Molly and Jake.

The Cornfield

It was a beautiful late summer's day and all the bushes and grasses around our ditch were alive with insects collecting pollen and nectar from the numerous blossom, for insects it was a busy time of the year.

The large cornfield that was very close outside our front door was ripe and ready for harvesting, there was plenty to eat there as the corn was falling from its husks onto the ground, and it was also a very nice place to play. 'Let's go outside and play in the corn' shouted Rosie. 'Ok' I said and we hopped from our house up the bank to the edge of the cornfield. 'Don't be too long!' shouted Mum. 'Your dinner will soon be ready!', 'Ok!' I shouted.

As we were about to enter the corn, Mr. Twitcher and elder and very wise rabbit said 'Be careful in the corn today, its days like this that humans do very strange things', he twitched his nose so much his glasses nearly fell off and then he hopped away.

Rosie ran into the corn. We played hide and seek together, running, jumping, chasing! We were having a lovely time, but it was a very hot day and we became very tired, so we decided to lay down on the soft warm ground and we fell fast asleep.

Suddenly Rosie jumped up! 'Oh Roy what is that awful noise and strong smell', with that the ground started to tremble and quiver. Rosie and I were very frightened, so we held each other very close as the noise and shaking got worse, Rosie started to cry.

I couldn't understand it, there were no other animals anywhere, and we were quite alone 'Let's get out of here' said Rosie, but I could still hear Mr. Twitcher's words ringing in my ears 'On days like this, humans do very strange things', so I grabbed Rosie's hand and ran towards the loud noise, as we got nearer we peaked out through the corn, there were four large machines driving round the field cutting the corn, my cousin told me they were combine harvesters and were very dangerous.

No wonder there were no animals about, because we were asleep we didn't hear the danger alarm call, now there was no escape and the field was getting smaller and smaller. 'Don't cry Rosie' I said, but I knew mum would be so worried and I felt like crying myself. We sat down in the middle of what was left of the cornfield.

Suddenly, everything went very quiet. I looked at Rosie and we crept to the edge of the corn and peered out, what we saw made us feel relief, the humans had stopped to have their lunch. This was our chance! We crept out of the corn and looked towards our ditch, we could see Mr. Twitcher with Mum and the rest of our neighbours lined up across the bank calling us. So we made a dash for home, but we never realised that the humans had dogs with them! So we began the greatest chase our little community had ever seen!

The dogs never caught us, all those times playing hide and seek really came in handy, we dashed to the ditch and everyone was cheering. We ran straight indoors and sat down exhausted, Mum came and gave us a big kiss and cuddles and said 'well the next time someone gives you advice , I think you better take it, you were both very lucky today' Mum was right of course so we went to bed very tired, but very happy.

The Visit

'Roy! , Rosie!' shouted Mum, to her two children 'Can you come in and get ready please!', Mrs Rabbit was going to take Roy and Rosie on a visit to see their auntie right across the other side of the big sunshine meadow. Auntie Beaty was very old and very bossy, Roy and Rosie were not fond of visiting her, but they did get to see their friends and get to play near Farmer Browns big pond.

It was a hot afternoon, Mrs Rabbit, Roy and Rosie shut their front door and started to walk along the ditch towards the sunshine meadow.

'Good afternoon Mrs Rabbit!' said Mr. Twitcher the wise rabbit. 'Afternoon Mr Twitcher' said Mrs Rabbit. 'It seems very quiet today Mrs Rabbit, the sky seems heavy and it's very sticky outside, so be careful in the ditches', 'we will' said Roy and Rosie.

After the strange, but often occurring greet with Mr. Twitcher, they left their ditch and they were now out in the open, not a very good place for the rabbits to be. They had to make their way to another ditch that ran along the sunshine meadow, they were nearly there until, the sky became very dark.

'Hurry you two! It's going to rain' said Mrs Rabbit. The sky got darker and darker, and then suddenly a very loud clap of thunder and bright lightening shot across the sky. Mrs Rabbit, Roy and Rosie were very frightened, then the rain started, it was light at first, but then it poured and started to fill the ditch the poor little rabbits were in. Roy and Rosie managed to keep clear of the rising water and scrambled to the top of the bank, but poor Mrs Rabbit wasn't quick enough, a log that was floating in the fast water, knocked her in! She floated past Roy and Rosie with speed 'Keep your head above the water Mum!' yelled Roy, but Mrs Rabbit was swept further away and around a bend.

Roy and Rosie ran along the field trying to keep up with poor Mrs Rabbit. Suddenly they saw her! She was stuck on a branch of a tree right in the middle of all the gushing water, how they were going to reach her before she got cold was the least of their worries.

Then by chance, along came Bill and Reg the water rat boys, who come from the same ditch as Roy and Rosie. Roy quickly explained what had happened to the rat boys, Bill and Reg are always swimming in Farmer Browns pond, so they dove into the water and swan quickly to unhook Mrs Rabbit from the branch and swam with her back to the bank.

Roy and Rosie helped Mrs Rabbit out of the water. 'Oh! Thank you Bill and Reg!' said Rosie and Roy, 'We can manage things from here', 'No problem' said Bill and Reg, incredibly in sync with each other, 'See you later Roy' and they went on their way.

The rain had stopped now and the sun was getting ready to shine, Mrs Rabbit was drying nicely and feeling much better, 'Come you two' she said 'Let's go home, we have had enough adventure for today, lets have a nice cup of tea and a big piece of carrot cake.

The Spring

Poor Mr. Twitcher had been very ill all winter, at one stage Mrs Rabbit was very worried about him, but everybody fussed over Mr. Twitcher, keeping him warm and fetching his food and it kept him quite cheerful, but Mr. Twitcher knew something was about to happen and it seemed to happen quite quick.

Roy and Rosie were not happy with the first winter of their short lives and wished it would hurry up and come to an end, but Mrs Rabbit said 'It just doesn't become summer, it creeps up on you very slowly', this is what she was told years ago by her father and sure enough this was exactly what was happening.

One winter's morning, the sun was shining so Roy and Rosie got up, got dressed and told Mrs Rabbit that they were going to see Mr. Twitcher. As they shut the front door something seemed, different somehow, the sun seemed warmer and there on the bushes were the first little leaf buds.

Pete the Pigeon was perched on a branch and he looked joyful as he said 'It's on it's way you know, summer is not far away, now it will come slowly, but it won't be long'. Roy and Rosie were very happy as they danced along to Mr. Twitchers.

Mr. Twitcher was up and singing 'It's a lovely day today' he sprung into the air and sang 'And my young nephew is coming to see me!', Roy and Rosie were pleased at the news because they liked Charlie and they always had an adventure when he was about.
It was late afternoon when there was a knock on Roy and Rosie's door. Rosie opened the door and there stood Charlie 'Come in!' said Mrs Rabbit, they were all so pleased to see him.

Charlie said it was the first day of Spring and that it was on the first night of Spring that the fairies had a meeting at the big fairy tree, so they all planned to go and see them. Come nightfall Roy Rosie and Charlie ran along the side of the field keeping very quiet, they settled in some long grass near the big tree and waited. After what seemed a long time they were all getting bored, hungry and cold, but then Charlie said 'Be quiet'. They looked into the black night and saw little lanterns of light; it was fairies going to the meeting.

They were very small with tiny wings and they were carrying tiny lanterns high in the air to shine their way. Roy, Rosie and Charlie were hesitant to move, as more fairies arrived until the gathering totalled about two hundred, all chatting in a funny language, suddenly everything all went quiet.

Roy, Charlie and Rosie looked at the night sky again to see, floating down onto a branch of the tree, King Ferdinand the Third, King of the fairies, he was about to say something when there was a terrible scream! It was Rosie her leg had gone stiff from sitting there so long and was in terrible pain. All the fairies fled never to return, Charlie mentioned that once the fairies had been discovered they never return to that place again.

And so the three adventurers set off home.

'I'm sorry' said Rosie, 'Oh it doesn't matter' said Roy and Charlie 'summer will soon be here and that will be even more exciting!' said Charlie.

Roy and Rosie told Mum about it, but they soon washed and cleaned their teeth and were asleep in no time.

The Big Escape

Roy and Rosie were very tired as they plodded along the field home. They had a lovely day, it was warm, they had eaten a lot and like all young rabbits they had played 'chase me' until they could run no more. As they were both passing some bushes, a young rabbit called to them, it was molly rabbit.

Molly rabbit lived in a ditch not far from Roy and Rosie, Rosie knew Molly and liked her very much 'Keep quiet and bob down' whispered Molly, so the two rabbits bobbed down in the underground by Molly rabbit and there in front of them stood a big red fox and he was looking for his dinner. The rabbits knew to be very quiet and still because young rabbits were the Fox's favourite dinner.

Roy and Rosie had never seen a fox close up before and they were quite frightened by him, he looked very mean and very hungry. Suddenly they heard a strange sound in the distance, it went 'Toot toot ...toot', the rabbits had never heard that sound before, but the fox certainly had because his ears shot up! And he then looked very frightened.

Then the rabbits found out what was making that strange noise, there were humans on horses, all wearing red coats galloping across Farmer Browns ploughed field and at their heels, lots and lots of dogs. The fox turned and ran as fast as he could across the field followed by the humans and the dogs. 'Cor! That was close' said Molly, but they still had to keep down until all the humans and the dogs were gone. When all was clear Molly Rabbit stated 'That

was called a fox hunt, humans like to do that sort of thing and it certainly saved us!'

Rosie and Roy said goodbye to their friend and thanked her for warning them, when they got home they told Mum all about it, Mum said it was all part of the dangers of being a rabbit, then she said that if Molly hadn't of seen Roy and Rosie then they would have walked right into the Fox.

They realised how lucky they had been and decided to make Molly a big carrot cake.

When Roy and Rosie were in bed ready to sleep
Rosie said 'Do you think that fox got away Roy?',
'I don't think so Rosie', but they were both glad it
was not them.

Roy was learning allot about his life around the
ditch and this will definitely help him when he's a
grown rabbit.

'I wonder what will happen tomorrow' said Rosie,
Roy rolled over and said goodnight.

The Big Tree

At the far end of our ditch stood a very large tree, it was the largest tree anywhere around for miles, it was a place we could play because it had large roots sticking out of the ground. It was the best place to play 'chase me' all the rabbit's favourite game. It was raining when we all got up, it was quite miserable actually and the sky was grey 'The sky is getting darker' said Mum, 'There could be a storm, so don't stray too far' she said.

The storm came as me and Roy were tidying our bedroom, lightening lit up the dark grey sky! Followed but the big roars of thunder which frightened me, 'Thunder doesn't hurt you Rosie' said Mum 'It's just the noise of the lightening'. Suddenly there was an ear splitting sound and a big streak of lightening followed hurtling across our ditch and hit the big tree.

Every animal living around the ditch felt the ground shake, but no-one dared look outside. When the storm passed all the families in the ditch looked out of their doors in amazement, there was the big tree lying across Farmer Browns newly ploughed field, the trunk of the tree was still smoking from where the lightening had struck!

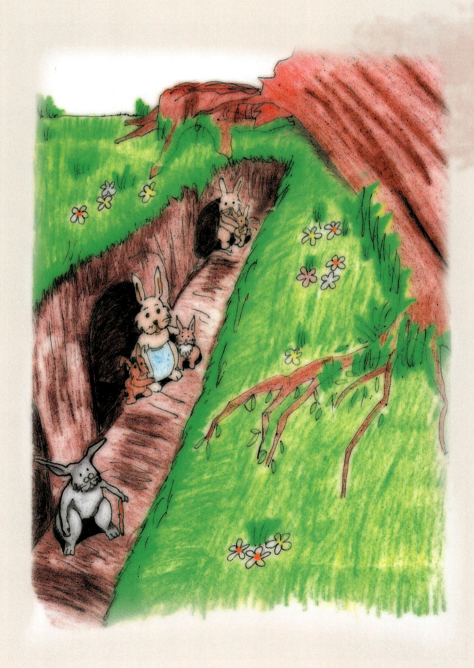

It was a humongous tree, animals came from far and wide to see the tree damage, but for some it was a time of plenty because there were millions of young green acorns to eat, tender green shoots and leaves that were at the top of the tree and even now it was a lovely place to play.

When all the animals had their fill of food and we were all tired from playing, Mr. Twitcher gathered all of us together, he said that soon there would be danger, the humans will come and cut up the tree with saws and tractors and take it away, so we were to be very careful.

Sure enough the humans came with their tractors and big saws and cut the tree into logs. The racket and the sound of working were tremendous! And we had to keep well hidden for three days. Slowly but surely the tree disappeared and everything was once again left to the animals. It was very exciting while it lasted, our ditch didn't seem the same after that.

'Of course!' said Roy to me and Mum, 'Aunty Beaty will never be able to find us, because that was the only landmark there was!', with that we all laughed and went to bed happy, it was nice living in our ditch and we were beginning to understand things a bit more, as we were slowly growing.

The Rainbow

It was pouring with rain and the sun was also shining, this seemed very strange to Roy and Rosie, suddenly something appeared in the sky that struck both little rabbits with awe. Right across the sky appeared a bond of beautiful colours, they were so amazed that they ran to Mr. Twitchers house, he would surly know what it was, him being so wise an all.

They arrived at Mr. Twitchers all excited and out of breath, trying to talk bolt at the same time 'Now slow down' said Mr. Twitcher, 'Come on in' he said closing the door behind us. Molly and Charlie were already there too.

Roy and Rosie explained about the rain and the sun shining at the same time, then they explained the colours that arched across the sky. Molly and Charlie were also very interested, so they all looked out of the window and sure enough the colours were still there!

'Now sit down all of you' said Mr. Twitcher and then he explained to the four little rabbits that the colours in the sky were called a rainbow, he also explained that rainbows only appeared when the rain and sun shined together, why he did not know, but he then said that if you find the end of a rainbow you could have anything you ever wished for. The four little rabbits looked at each other. 'Oh!' they all said, 'what a lovely adventure that will make!' Rosie said.

Roy, Rosie, Molly and Charlie were now outside and looking at the rainbow, to break the silence Rosie then said 'Looks to me, the end of the rainbow is in Farmer Browns big field', 'Yes!' said the others 'Let's go and find it!'. 'When we find it' said Roy 'I want a giant carrot cake all to myself', 'yeah me too!' said Charlie. Molly and Rosie wanted silly girly things as usual.

They set off all excited, creeping along the ditch they went towards the open of a small wood near Farmer Browns field, 'What are you lot up to?' asked Mrs Moorhen , 'We are looking for the end of the rainbow' said Roy, Mrs Moorhen smiled and walked away pecking at the ground.

The four adventurers crept to the edge of the small wood, and then ran to the open of the field, but there was no rainbow, it seemed to have moved. 'Come on!' Charlie said eagerly 'This way!', and so they were chasing the rainbow all day, but never found the end. When the rainbow disappeared they plodded back to Mr. Twitchers house very disappointed. 'Oh' said Mr. Twitcher 'You never found the end of the rainbow?', 'every time we thought we had it, it moved' said Charlie.

'My my' said Mr. Twitcher 'if it was as easy as that, we would all be rich, wouldn't we? And there would be nothing to look forward to in life' Mr. Twitcher was right of course, he always was, that is what makes him so wise.

Roy and Rosie plodded home for dinner, they explained everything to Mrs Rabbit, who then said 'what you four did today was another lesson in growing up, not to be greedy and want everything at once, one day you will be as wise as Mr. Twitcher and learn to take things as they come, that is the rabbits way'

Roy and Rosie went to bed and Mrs Rabbit brought them both a nice piece of carrot cake each. 'thank you mum' they both said. 'Well Roy it's not a whole carrot cake, but we must have been somewhere near the end of that rainbow to get just a slice' said Rosie, they laughed, ate their cake and fell fast asleep.

Lightning Source UK Ltd.
Milton Keynes UK
UKIC03n0057130217
294236UK00003B/11